3 Great Offers MR. MEN Fans!

KU-021-262

3 Sixteen Beautiful Fridge Magnets – any 2 for £2.00!

inc.P&P

They're very special collector's items!
Simply tick your first and second* choices from the list below
of any 2 characters!

1st Choice

- [ ] Mr. Happy
- [ ] Mr. Lazy
- [ ] Mr. Topsy-Turvy
- [ ] Mr. Bounce
- [ ] Mr. Bump
- [ ] Mr. Small
- [ ] Mr. Snow
- [ ] Mr. Wrong

- [ ] Mr. Daydream
- [ ] Mr. Tickle
- [ ] Mr. Greedy
- [ ] Mr. Funny
- [ ] Little Miss Giggles
- [ ] Little Miss Splendid
- [ ] Little Miss Naughty
- [ ] Little Miss Sunshine

2nd Choice

- [ ] Mr. Happy
- [ ] Mr. Lazy
- [ ] Mr. Topsy-Turvy
- [ ] Mr. Bounce
- [ ] Mr. Bump
- [ ] Mr. Small
- [ ] Mr. Snow
- [ ] Mr. Wrong

- [ ] Mr. Daydream
- [ ] Mr. Tickle
- [ ] Mr. Greedy
- [ ] Mr. Funny
- [ ] Little Miss Giggles
- [ ] Little Miss Splendid
- [ ] Little Miss Naughty
- [ ] Little Miss Sunshine

*Only in case your first choice is out of stock.

--- TO BE COMPLETED BY AN ADULT ---

To apply for any of these great offers, ask an adult to complete the coupon below and send it with the appropriate payment and tokens, if needed, to MR. MEN OFFERS, PO BOX 7, MANCHESTER M19 2HD

- [ ] Please send ____ Mr. Men Library case(s) and/or ____ Little Miss Library case(s) at £5.99 each inc P&P
- [ ] Please send a poster and door hanger as selected overleaf. I enclose six tokens plus a 50p coin for P&P
- [ ] Please send me ____ pair(s) of Mr. Men/Little Miss fridge magnets, as selected above at £2.00 inc P&P

Fan's Name _____

Address _____

_____ **Postcode** _____

Date of Birth _____

Name of Parent/Guardian _____

Total amount enclosed £ _____

- [ ] **I enclose a cheque/postal order payable to Egmont Books Limited**
- [ ] **Please charge my MasterCard/Visa/Amex/Switch or Delta account** (delete as appropriate)

Card Number

Expiry date ___/___   **Signature** _____

Please allow 28 days for delivery. We reserve the right to change the terms of this offer at any time but we offer a 14 day money back guarantee. This does not affect your statutory rights.

CUT ALONG DOTTED LINE AND RETURN THIS WHOLE PAGE

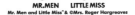

MR.MEN   LITTLE MISS
Mr. Men and Little Miss™ & ©Mrs. Roger Hargreaves

MR. SMALL
a big day out

Original concept by Roger Hargreaves
Illustrated and written by Adam Hargreaves

MR. MEN   LITTLE MISS

Mr Small was out for a walk.

He was feeling more than a little sorry for himself.

It wasn't much fun being as small as he was.

He sat down under a tree and closed his eyes.

"I do so wish I was bigger," he sighed.

"Much, much bigger," he added.

Now, Mr Small did not know that there was a wizard lying down on the other side of the tree.

He had stopped for a snooze and, just as he had been dozing off, the wizard had overheard Mr Small's wish.

The wizard smiled to himself.

Without even opening his eyes, he muttered some magic words under his breath and then went back to sleep.

As Mr Small lay there, something really quite remarkable happened.

Something really quite remarkably magic.

Mr Small began to grow.

And grow.

And grow.

Until he bumped his head on a branch!

When he crawled out from underneath the tree and stood up he was taller than the tree.

Much taller.

"Gosh," said Mr Small.

He could not believe his eyes.

He could not believe his size!

He went for a walk to try out his new size.

It was wonderful.

He could see over the top of everything.

He leap-frogged over trees and jumped over rivers.

He gave Mr Uppity the shock of his life.

He was stronger than Mr Strong.

Noisier than Mr Noisy.

And taller than Mr Tall!

He could even make his fingers meet when he put his arms around Mr Greedy's tummy!

Mr Small had a marvellous day, and as the sun set he lay down in a field and went to sleep.

As Mr Small slept he shrank back to his normal size.

For you see, the wizard had only cast a spell that would last one day.

When Mr Small woke up it was dark.

"What a wonderful dream," he said to himself, and got up to walk home.

But he found he couldn't. He was surrounded by a wall!

However, when he felt along the bottom, he discovered that he could lift up the wall.

It was light outside, and when he crawled out Mr Small could not believe his eyes.

He had been trapped underneath a hat!

A hat that looked just like his own, but it was much, much bigger.

"Well, I never," said Mr Small. "Maybe it wasn't a dream after all."

That sleepy old wizard had forgotten to finish off his spell properly.

He had forgotten to make sure Mr Small's hat had shrunk back to the right size.

Mr Small now had a ten-gallon hat.

A ten-gallon hat for a pint-sized person!